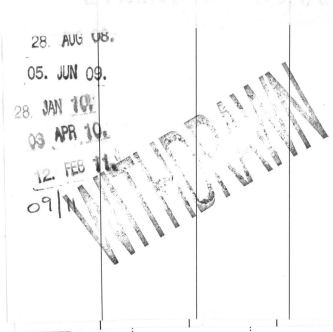

THE PERSIAN POMEGRANATE

AND OTHER SHORT STORIES

THE
PERSIAN
POMEGRANATE

AND OTHER SHORT STORIES

William N. Vellacott

IMAGES
PUBLISHING

Published in Great Britain 1995 by
Images Publishing (Malvern) Ltd.,
Upton-Upon-Severn,
Worcestershire.

British Library Cataloguing in Publication Data

A catalogue record for this book is available
from the British Library

ISBN 1 897817 56 8

Set in Gatineau 10pt

Designed and Produced by Images Publishing (Malvern) Ltd.
Printed and Bound in Great Britain by Bookcraft, Bath, Avon.

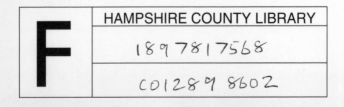

Contents

LEAVES

These leaves that rustle faintly underfoot
Have felt the joy of moving in the wind,
Have stretched themselves so lithely 'gainst the tug
And strain and romping riot of the skies,
And whispered back their welcome to the sun.
Like little boys they've hated to be washed.
Subdued and sorrowful beneath the rain
They've waited and have wept,
Then shaken off their wetness for the flowers
Growing open-mouthed below for all the hours.
If survival can't be gained some other way,
Then perhaps I'd like to be a leaf one day!

Styx

Adam saw quite clearly that he had only a few moments to live, and that he must make the most of them. After all, they timed athletes down to a hundredth of a second, and he had over a hundred such periods to play with.

First, he must deal with the young idiot who, on a corner with walls on either side, had pulled out to pass a lorry, and was about to have a head-on with his own heavy saloon.

As a youngster he had himself, more than once, taken a similar gamble with happy and excited abandon, and without a thought for the possible involvement of any but himself.

He had been lucky; this young man was not.

So, with an effort he had not needed to make for years, he fought off an instant hatred of his slayer, and pushed aside the ready contempt of the mature for the relentless, natural egotism of youth.

Understanding and a slow forgiveness passed into his gaze, and he was rewarded by the shadow of a smile in the young eyes ahead of him.

Adam tucked that smile into his belt and knew that, at least on this rather important occasion, he had not entirely failed in his relations with his fellow men.

He had sometimes wondered what would go through one's mind at the final countdown. Would there be some brilliant revelation, perhaps some last certainty of survival or non-survival which had eluded him during fifty years on earth? He had doubted it, and was pleased to find that he did not now even wish for such a revelation.

What he thought he wanted was a recollection of the more important moments of his life if he could only decide what these were; and if possible a knitting of them together to form some sort of spiritual garment suitable for any type of journey, if indeed any such journey was forthcoming.

A childhood dialogue came to mind.

"I won't!"

"You will!"

"Won't!"

Adam could not now remember what he would not give her, but the shock of the little girl's slap across his face which followed his second refusal had remained with him vividly.

His father cuffed him occasionally. That a girl should cuff him was bewildering. He had never seen his mother do this to his father, nor any female to any male, but obviously it occurred, and he must cope with it as best he could.

He had seen amusement and then contempt grow in the girl's eyes as she watched him struggling with his problem. This would never do. If she behaved like a boy she must be treated as one.

He hit her as she had hit him, and saw dismay displace contempt, and the proud little face crumple into tears.

Feeling both elated and miserable he watched her run off home. "Dad," he asked his father that evening when tucked up in bed, "Sheila hit me today when I would not give her something she wanted. I hit her back. Was that right?"

9

His father laughed gently. "I'm afraid not, son. It's a case of words only when you disagree with a lady. Why? I suppose because they're usually regarded as weaker creatures."

"But she's stronger than me, more than a year older." "Well," replied his father a little helplessly, "perhaps it was not so bad for you to hit her back."

So that was how it was.

Even adults, even one's own dad, did not really know what was right, and what was not. No rules were reliable, not one was to be trusted as final and unalterable. Life suddenly became much more difficult, and much more interesting. Of course, he thought with a happy feeling of understanding, I must make my own rules, slowly, painfully, little by little, moving towards a day when I shall know with certainty how to behave in any set of circumstances, perhaps even in the face of death.

To his vexation, pleasant trivialities crowded upon him. He could not resist a chuckle as one of his favourite stories came to mind: the despairing missionary, pursued by the inevitable lion, was falling to his knees and praying to his God. The animal, also on his knees, and also praying to his God, looked up at the missionary, "I don't know what you can be doing," he said severely, "but I'm saying grace!" And Adam was just conscious of a wistful wish that he too, like the missionary, and like the lion, could turn sincerely to his God and seek his blessing.

Memories raced towards him: of the face of his first love, sensitive, serene, a little freckled indeed, but with an enchanting radiance which had moved him as no other face had ever done; of his daughter, aged about five, throwing herself into his arms with a passion of affection after he had been away for a day or two; and of a walk with wife, children and the family dog on his favourite bit of England, those ten surprising miles of the Malvern Hills, with their slim crest of grassy granite, with views, east and west, not soon forgotten, and where a fine poet had written, and a famous musician composed; happy recollections, but not quite what he was looking for.

Less pleasing memories arrived on the scene. "Why can't you marry me?" a girl was asking.

"Because you are not exactly the right person, and I should make a mess of it."

"And it has taken you over three years to find out?

11

It's a long garden path to be led along, Adam."

Yes, and he had not hesitated to gather flowers on the way. "There's somebody else," the girl had gone on with quiet conviction. And indeed she was right.

He thought with humility of the many men and women, so very many it seemed, whose qualities he had admired because he lacked them himself, and had wished it was not so.

And then at last it came to him.

This, here and now, was the most important moment of his life. Not because it was about to end, but because, in the face of the final provocation by a fellow human being, he had reached something approaching selflessness, and was not bitter that he should need to pay with his life for this achievement.

Just why this was so important he could not fathom, and had not the time to ponder. He had to be content with being certain that it was so.

He met the boy's eyes again, closer this time, and exchanged a friendly look which had its due elements of gravity, of resignation, and of comradeship in the ultimate adventure.

Tea with Cake

About the little courts and cloisters of a famous abbey are a number of dwellings. In some of these, men who have served the Abbey well may end their days as peacefully as in the quietest village in England.

In one such dwelling, on one side of what has been called the oldest garden in Britain, sat an elderly man, scanty-haired, highly coloured, and with eyes of as deep a blue as one was likely to find. He was dressed in comfortable garments suitable for a retired clergyman, but yet allowing him to attend evening service with a minimum of adjustment.

"Uncle!" came from a vigorous, bearded and somewhat intense young man talking between mouthfuls of cherry cake, "I've been doing my very best to shock you for most of half an hour now, and all I've managed to produce is the most sympathetic, most amiable of smiles from that enigmatic face of yours."

A sobering thought struck him.

"Don't tell me you were saying the same sort of thing to your uncle forty or so years ago?"

"Not quite the same, but on the other hand not very different, I think."

The lad loosened his sweater at the neck, and confronted the bewildering possibility that his splendid ideas were not so fresh and original as he had supposed.

"Do you mean to say that you also told him you could get along just as well without as with a God? That it's quite impossible to respect a God who seems to need and demand worship and praise, and indeed to wallow in both? That asking forgiveness of him is absurdly irrational? My many sins have been committed against people, and it is their forgiveness I could do with."

"My very dear boy," came back gently, "do consider that total uncritical belief in anything whatever is quite uncalled for, and is indeed frustrating, and suitable only for saints and zealots."

The old gentleman thought very carefully for a moment or two. "Perhaps it will do no harm if I manage to surprise you just a little. Let us take a look at the possibility, or likelihood, or certainty of any future life when this one is done. The evidence in favour would hardly survive the onslaught of any efficient barrister for more than a matter of minutes. A good scientist would be reduced to despair in an effort to support it. Even the miracles do not seem quite to tip the balance. And yet there is this strange wonder and beauty about this man's dramatic message.

"It seems quite often to achieve a faith and a conviction not easily toppled even by common sense, and all that lack of evidence. And I must admit that the idea of a possible life ahead grows less and less important to me as my days grow fewer. And that feeling does not make me unhappy. Rather the reverse, for I have no anxiety about it now."

Surprise and pleasure silenced Paul for a while.

"But don't you feel rather a hypocrite?" and he gazed round the book-lined room, through the mullioned windows into the garden on whose lawn men had paced to and fro for so long, pondering such subjects.

The blue eyes twinkled merrily for a moment, and then grew serious.

"No man, I think, need accept all of any religion, for

that may involve him in stresses which can only do harm. I doubt if there has ever lived more than a handful of perfect Christians since the time of the founder. Even that founder himself had great difficulty on occasions in living up to his own ideals. And his last sad words even make me wonder if he began to doubt his own divinity."

They were silent for a time, and Paul, wondering if this was the moment to ask his big question, looked anxiously at the Uncle who had been his much-loved guardian, guide and friend since his parents had died when he was a child.

He rose from his chair and looked out onto the lawn.

"I want to get married; to an African girl, daughter of one of the staff of the Nigerian High Commission. Would you marry us, Uncle?"

He watched the steady eyes, and noticed now no twinkle there. "Let us take a stroll," the old man suggested, and they moved out into the walled garden, the City's traffic just a summer murmur towards the river.

"As a young man, City trained, and with no thought of becoming a priest," he went on slowly, "I was sent by the Bank which employed me to open a branch at

Bangkok. Fascinated by Buddhism, by its exotic Temples, and by the lively people of that country, I fell in love with a local girl and married her. We lived near the river, and I got to know those complex waterways, bubbling with floating households, as well as I know the City of London. No doubt I should have stayed, but I was ambitious and, when offered promotion, I brought her to London."

Paul waited impatiently, and even kicked a blade or two from the precious turf.

"You know," his Uncle continued, not yet quite ready to commit himself to a decision, "Buddha's Way of Life might suit you in some ways, for a time. He taught that the Universe is far beyond human understanding; he bothered little about God, or theology, and did not concern himself with faith, or worship, or praise, or even prayer. And he was silent regarding any future life, and painted no rosy picture of Paradise, or Nirvana as he called it."

"But surely he thought rebirth an important part of his religion," objected Paul, both impatient and interested, "and there's no shred of evidence to support that."

"Suffering in India, then as now," his Uncle resumed

quietly, "was very marked. Hunger, disease, intense poverty, early death were the fate of most. The Hindus, brilliant and creative as ever, thought of rebirth long before Buddha's time. For them, its offer of spiritual and perhaps material growth was the most satisfactory explanation of this unequal, senseless suffering. I believe Buddha could think of nothing better, and adopted it too."

Paul replaced a divot he had kicked from the lawn.

"But you grow irritable, and did not expect a sermon for your tea." Something approaching a smile brought back a personal warmth to the conversation.

"Will you marry us, Uncle?" Paul repeated.

"Most races, Hindus, Jews, Arabs, and many others, prefer a man to marry his own kind," the old man went on. "The English as much as any. If he doesn't, well, they let him know their feelings about it, and his wife too; indeed they do; or indeed they did."

"And what happened in your case?"

"My wife was profoundly unhappy. She stood it for a year or two, then returned to her own family. I've not seen her since, and barely thought of her for thirty years."

"Am I to learn a lesson from this?"

They walked back slowly to the house, and as they entered the room the blue eyes lit up with what Paul had always thought the most friendly smile in all the world.

"I rather hope so. But I do not expect it. Things are much changed on this subject, perhaps for the better. But

I am too old to change with them, and would not wish to."

That evening at Evensong, Paul's Uncle prayed sincerely to his Maker for forgiveness.

He very seldom lied, and hoped that on this occasion he might be forgiven.

And indeed he had so very nearly married that lovely girl those many years ago.

———— ❧ ————

Sunday Morning

In the small church of a very small Dorset village, a mile or two from the sea, the congregation at the 11 o'clock matins service rarely swells beyond a score.

On the other hand, it even more rarely sinks far below double figures. And on the two or three great occasions of the Christian year, the farmers arrive in family droves, extra seats fill nave and sides aisles, and the old church vibrates with the roar of lusty country voices.

The porch is rather narrow, and the first necessity is to squeeze past the portly bell-ringer without upsetting the rhythm of the single cheerful bell.

Church bells are allowed great liberties in the matter of time-keeping, but not in those cases where there is but one of them. The worthy ringer is well aware of this, and on that unfortunate occasion when I so carelessly tripped on a mat and clutched at the nearest figure for support, all eight heads in the congregation turned to survey the situation with a precision acceptable at the Colour Trooping on Horse Guards Parade.

When the bell had reasserted itself, the heads slowly resumed their normal position, and their owners concluded that the unusual word they thought they had heard was indeed that word and no other, but that in the circumstances a single eruption, however colourful, showed admirable restraint in their man at the bell.

This particular winter morning was really very chilly, and the two single-bar electric heaters far away among the rafters may have brought comfort to a small family of spiders, but not very much to mortals away down on the earth.

So my arrival, provided I avoided knocking the gentleman down again, was awaited with anxious anticipation. This was because a local resident, not long deceased, from pneumonia we understand, had bequeathed to the church her venerable Super Ser heater, and two gas cylinders. From years of painful practice with my own Super Ser, I had learned which way to twist a certain lever, and in what order to press certain knobs, with suitable hesitations while it coughed and spluttered.

The congregation had not exactly gathered round the Super Ser, but its disposition suggested a feeling of sympathy towards the apparatus. As guardian of the almost sacred flame, I was expected to sit as near to it as possible, and this privilege I enjoyed to the full.

The bell quiet, the flame lit and hissing gently, attention was now directed towards the vestry door, from which came little puffy noises as the large and severely arthritic vicar struggled into his vestments, gathered his stick, and tapped his way slowly and firmly down the stone-flagged nave. There had been thefts from churches in the vicinity, and his affectionate parishioners would sometimes allow themselves to speculate on the well-being of any would-be thief whom the vicar thought might be taking an interest in the church plate.

They might even permit themselves, just for a moment, an extravagant vision of the vicar, at an earlier stage in his career, hurling himself at a pair of legs in his famous international rugby tackle of fifty years before.

The service flowed along like a broad, deep river. The vicar, with his fine voice assisted here and there by a murmur from the little organ, carried his flock along past familiar prayers and responses, a psalm, and a cheerful hymn to the first lesson. This he read very slowly and carefully, almost as though he was himself paying close attention to the words for the first time.

Another hymn, and he sank quietly out of sight as he handed over command to the Brigadier for the reading of the second lesson. This was done with both bark and bite, and no complaint of inaudibility was ever made from the very hardest of hearing. And even when they were not there, one tended to look for the splendid array of medals which glittered once a year on his manly frontage. On Remembrance Sunday, at 11 a.m., they were there by the war memorial for all to see. And taking a long look at what was known as 'the Brig's basinful of brass' had for many a year been one of the pleasures permitted to every child in the village.

A further hymn, a short sermon with the lesson he had read as his subject, a few more prayers, and the final offertory hymn was at hand. This was linked to one little problem which was always solved before the service began. The two bags were carried by a rather small husband and an even smaller wife; Medical Missionaries, they had spent a lifetime on a remote Indonesian island.

It seemed impossible that either had ever done anything that was not shared equally with the other, and it was quite unacceptable that any such thing should happen now. The congregation tended, as we know, to sit on the warmer side of the church, where the stove was, but one or two always moved discreetly across if it seemed that husband or wife might bear an empty bag to the altar.

The service completed, the blessing given, and minds perhaps almost ready to dwell lightly on the Sunday roast, the vicar walked to the vestry, humming the little tune which always came to him at such moments. There, one or another of the ladies took her weekly turn, jealously guarded, to aid the old man's arthritic fingers with the removal of vestments.

Up at the altar a vigorous, heavily bearded young churchwarden, the local schoolmaster, busied himself. His ancestors had, for generations, used the many local coves and inlets for the successful smuggling of wine and brandy, tobacco and silks from the little French ports across the water. This in no way hindered his standing with his pupils, some few of whom had similar proud connections with the past.

He tidied things away, and carried back to the vestry that portion of the heavy Braille bible which had been used for the reading of the first lesson.

For our vicar, of course, is quite blind.

Slit Trench

After three men in Headquarter Company, and finally the Regimental Sergeant Major had been caught by this particularly accurate sniper, the Colonel suddenly lost his temper.

"I'm going to destroy that bloody man," he said angrily, "I know just where he is. Tell Graham to bring up my carrier at once."

Nobody tried to dissuade him. Nobody ever did. And yet this was an especially rash and hazardous undertaking for anyone to consider, let alone an infantry battalion commander with the guiding reins of a fighting unit of a thousand men in his hands.

The battalion had moved forward two or three hundred yards during the night, and now, dug into their slit trenches in the North African sand, the soldiers were pinned down at dawn by some machine guns, and a sniper on a ridge ahead.

The Commanding Officer was the youngest Lieutenant Colonel in the Division. It is likely that he was also the most unpopular. He had taken over the battalion six weeks before with a fine record as a Company commander in the field. Within days the unit had changed from a reasonably efficient, reasonably effective fighting force to something quite different, and much less useful.

He had managed it in a simple and disastrous way. He let all ranks know, and continue to know, that they were about half as good at their particular job as he had expected them to be.

The Unit's first reaction was one of frank disbelief that any man could be quite so tactless. Then, after the battalion had taken a long and careful look at itself in the light of this critical judgement, a dull resentment began to smoulder and erupt.

The Doctor, Frank Arnold, trod his cheerful and amiable path with more than usual circumspection. He was an untidy, even slovenly soldier, but a conscientious Regimental Medical Officer. And his somewhat civilian attitude to soldiering was offset by his hobby which was rifle shooting. It was known, also, that at school he had won a certain prize at Bisley which suggested that his knowledge at least of small arms was considerable.

When Graham, driver of the Bren-gun carrier, arrived in his little tracked vehicle beside the C.O.'s slit trench he was understandably jittery. A hundred yards ahead of them were two burnt-out British tanks, part of the Armoured Division which the infantry battalion was supporting. Powerful 88 millimetre German anti-tank guns had destroyed them, and Graham understood very clearly that he was expected to take his carrier within easy range of the sniper, and provide both a firing platform for his commanding officer, and a simple if rather trivial target for the anti-tank guns. The C.O. was plainly taking the gamble that the enemy gun crews would be holding their ammunition for the British tanks. These were now safely hidden in dips in the sand, but would certainly attack sooner or later.

Frank watched from the Regimental Aid Post as the C.O. jumped from his slit trench and slid into the carrier. He flinched as he heard a bullet flatten itself within an inch or two of the man's head. Graham drove off with a jerk and those who knew what was afoot settled down to await the outcome.

The Doc gratefully accepted a mug of tea from his Sergeant and fidgeted with a cigarette as the minutes toiled by. Like the rest of them he thought of Graham, sweating profusely, as he drove the clanking carrier to the point from which the C.O. had decided to fire. And then of that deadly moment when the carrier would suddenly halt, and two men, each behind a weapon, would depend like any Western hero and villain on individual speed, skill and accuracy for survival. The Doc had an uncomfortable feeling that the odds were heavily on the sniper, a professional marksman lying un-hurried and cool and prepared, with telescopic sights on the best rifle available. More minutes passed.

Then there was a screech of brakes, the carrier loomed over the trench, and a body was hastily lowered into waiting arms.

"Couldn't keep his bloody head out of the way," came from Graham, infinitely relieved to be alive himself, and the vehicle moved briskly away.

It was, of course, the C.O. with a neat little entry wound to one side of his head. On the other, Frank found that the bullet lay just under the skin, having penetrated skull and brain. It was difficult to believe that this fine young face, so recently vigorous and now at last in repose, had completed its due spell of expression. And that there would be no further chance for this man to mature and check his blazing ambition and impetuosity, and develop the tact and warmth to which men will most readily respond.

Frank covered the entry wound with a tiny dressing, and looked with displeasure at the ugly swelling on the opposite side, marring the strong features. He reached for a scalpel, incised briefly, drew out the bullet and pulled the skin edges together with a piece of strapping. Then he cleaned the bullet, looked at it carefully, and slipped it into his pocket.

A few evenings later the Doc was standing by the sea, with the curved stone tiers of a decaying Roman theatre rising behind him. He felt rather too much like an actor at the end of a final scene, which indeed he was as he took an object from his pocket, looked at it quizzically for a moment, and then threw it far into the quiet Mediterranean sky. He watched it curve lazily till at last it disappeared, with an undignified plop and a momentary ripple, from the sight of man.

Frank pondered as he walked back slowly towards the little tent he had acquired recently as an item of loot. The bullet, distorted though it was, he was sure was a British one and had been fired from a British rifle. An unpleasant thought, but not quite as unpleasant as it sounded. For the opposing armies had chased each other to and fro along the coast several times, helping themselves to the choicest equipment left behind by the fleeing opposition; and using it when they were short, and when it happened to be preferable to their own. And Frank knew that the best of the British rifles was a good deal better than anything available to the Italians and Germans just then. Moreover, the entry wound had been nearer the front than the back of the head. And he thought with uncritical wonder of the half ashamed sigh of relief which had blown like a cleansing wind through the Regiment at this man's death. It discounted utterly, it seemed, the man's courage, and dedication, and promise.

He stopped once on his way, to pounce eagerly on a Roman coin among the pebbles. He then disappeared into his tent as night, with a proper sense of timing, abruptly fell.

Mum's the Word

"How do you manage with your mother-in-law about the place?" Paul asked his friends.

"Hardly notice she's there," came from one, "she only says a word or two about once a week."

"Couldn't do without her," said another with four children.

Paul was quite fond of Sarah's mum, a frank and cheerful soul with well-stocked conversational resources and great stamina.

But there were times when silence seemed as rare as summer snow, and much more desirable.

Paul spent a large portion of his time in his workshop in the yard. His was meticulous work needing careful concentration, and interruptions were just so much wasted time.

"You talk too much, much too much," he had said to

her once when she brought him morning coffee and stayed on to chatter of yesterday, today and tomorrow.

"I know, my dear. I always have, and I doubt if it will change. Do you know, dogs make the best listeners; cats just don't attend. One day I shall have three dogs, and keep them on an eight hour shift basis."

Family privacy. That was what he had enjoyed so much. To be able, for instance, to embrace your wife in the most outrageous situations; just as she was getting out of the bath, half-dried; in the middle of a telephone conversation with her friend in the house opposite; and on the rather steep stairs with her coming down and he waiting at the bottom, and able to caress her at his leisure from the so-shapely thighs to the much-loved wealth of chestnut hair.

These simple delights had gone for ever, he thought.

And perhaps the bitterest blow came when he realised, from something she let slip, that the lady could hear, through the unsubstantial wall between their bedrooms, every word he said in bed to Sarah. The world crumbled gently about his tingling ears as he remembered what some of those words had been.

Six months had now passed since the death of his

father-in-law, and Paul thought a cautious suggestion might be justified.

"Mum," he said to her one evening as they sat round a fire. "It's time you thought of marrying again. You're still quite young, as good looking as most men want, you've got a bit of money and you're a much merrier widow than most."

"But I talk too much; only dogs and the deaf can stand it, I'm afraid."

"Nonsense! Anyway, may I put an advert in a suitable newspaper, setting out the facts, and asking for interested parties? I could mention 'talkative', or 'sociable', and 'shapely lady', or whatever else you like."

"Well, I'll be damned!" she said, colouring and clutching for time to consider this outrageous proposal. For once she was happy to be quiet. "Well, well!" she went on after a long pause. "It might be interesting. I don't see much male company these days, now Mark has moved to a flat the other side of town. And perhaps a little competition wouldn't do him any harm just now."

Mark was Sarah's god-father and her late father's life-long friend. He had lodged with them as part of the family for as long as she could remember.

The advertisement was composed and duly appeared, resulting in a surprising array of masculine talent.

After much careful selection, with Mum making final decisions, the competitors were eventually reduced to three, and a tea-party was arranged.

It was really a considerable success. Mum certainly talked a great deal, and embarrassed silences were not a feature of the occasion. Sarah provided tea and cakes, and her mum took the precaution of adding half a dozen bottles of beer. Thus, when the gentlemen were not listening to her, they were soon quite happily talking to each other.

It was about half way through the beer when a ring was heard at the front door.

"That'll be Mark, I expect," she said to the company in general. "I was sure none of you would mind if I asked an old friend to join us. Paul and Sarah know him well, of course."

In no way damped by this addition, the party proceeded under Mum's firm guidance to the conclusion of the last glass of beer. Reluctant farewells were said, with perhaps a speculative warmth in a number of masculine eyes, and Mark was asked to stay on to supper.

"I've a word or two to say to you, young man," he said to Paul later when the two men were alone together, and Paul did not much care for the look on the rugged features turned towards him. Mark had generous whiskers and a healthy moustache. One side of this tended to vibrate when he spoke and the other remain still, a feature which Paul now found much less entertaining than on previous occasions.

"Were I a younger man," Mark went on slowly and distinctly, "I might do more than just talk to the chap who advertises my future wife, mother of my three children, as though she were one of too many kittens, or a puppy wanting a good home."

"Mother of your . . .?"

"Yes, I didn't mean to tell you, but now you know, see that it goes no further."

"Mother of your three . . .?"

"Quite right. The boys are in Canada, as you are aware. The girl you are lucky enough to have as your wife. Your late father-in-law and I were nippers together; we went to the same school, married twin sisters on the same day, and, not long after, the same shell injured my face and put paid to any chance of a family for him."

"Your own wife died, I think?"

"She was killed in one of the London air-raids, and after the war the three of us just settled down together. Very happy we've been, I think, and I'm sorry it's over."

"And now?"

"We shall be married in a month or two, I hope. That is, of course, if one of your customers hasn't pushed his nose in front. I'd better enquire. Would you ask her to come in."

Paul rose a little unsteadily, said "What a bloody fool I am" to no one in particular, and moved to the kitchen.

"He wants to know," he told his mother-in-law, "if he's still the favourite."

A little later he put his head round the door, and was not surprised to find the two of them happily engaged in a dialogue concerning dates and dresses, hats and honeymoons.

He withdrew hastily, but had sufficient time to notice that Mark was beginning gently but firmly to remove his hearing aid.

adre's
Progress

The battle for the small town of Modica, twenty miles south-east of Ragusa on the island of Sicily, was over. The Italians had pulled out, and exhausted British troops were beginning to look around for the least uncomfortable quarters they could find.

The battalion padre, wearing a green and white feather in his cap, sat on a bench and watched the men, many of whom he knew well. He always felt despondent and useless when the fighting was on. The wounded wanted to get to the doctor, the dying were either pre-occupied with their plight, or their minds were elsewhere and seldom interested in final regrets or changes of attitude. Of course he played his part in burying the dead, but that was about all.

Suddenly he realised a voice was questioning him.

"The Shop, mate, know where it is?" The Shop. That was the brothel of course. Even the padre got to know that sooner or later.

"No," he said sadly, "I'm afraid I cannot help you."

The soldier, startled by the accent, noticed the padre's rank and moved away.

So he couldn't even provide that small and valued piece of information. Perhaps next time he would see to it that he could do just that; just one useful thing. Then he laughed ruefully at the mildly ridiculous picture it presented to him.

He rose, sighed, and turned back to look for his batman who would, he knew, by now have found him a more or less comfortable place for the night.

It was some days later, in the little square of another little town, that a similar request was made by another soldier. It drew a different reply.

"Well now, so it's the brothel you're after. I'm told it's on the edge of the town. Here's a map, so we'd better find it together." The padre led the soldier past tables and chairs set carefully beneath the patient trees, across the square and down a side street as the warm evening darkened, and the townsfolk came from their houses into the streets to chatter of the day's events.

The houses had begun to thin out when the padre stopped before one with three orange trees before it. It had seen better days, but was of mellow old stone with a roof heavily tiled, and walls thickly clad with vines whose branches were beginning to sag with ripening fruit. The lower windows were shuttered and little light showed, but the door opened at once when the soldier knocked. He was briefly and expertly scanned by a middle-aged woman and invited in.

"Keep your eye on the time," the padre reminded him, "or you'll be in trouble." He spoke with less than his usual conviction as the drowsy scents of the little garden quickened his war-dimmed senses.

He had been aware of a dark head at an upper window, but it was gone now as he turned to leave. He had moved only a step or two when the door burst open and a slim young form, black haired and vivid, was upon him and had flung her arms round his neck.

"Sir, oh Sir!" the girl was in tears, and he patted her head awkwardly as she sobbed herself to silence.

"What is it, child?"

"I have heard no voice from home for so many, many months; it was the greatest delight to hear you just talking a few moments ago." And she sobbed afresh and clung to him.

He might have told her that for him too the sound of a girl's voice from his own country was a forgotten sweetness in whose toils he now found himself floundering; and that his careful – he had thought impregnable – defences had been caught unawares and scattered to the winds. He barely heard what she was saying.

"I came to this town two years ago to a good job with a nice family. They left suddenly three months ago, and were not able to take me with them. I could find no other work. I had no chance of getting home. I could not starve. What was I to do? What was I to do?"

He gently wiped her tears away, and stroked her warm cheeks. Eyes at first fearful, and then wide with wonder, she kissed him shyly and then with freedom as a little evening breeze, with delicate approval, blew lightly by.

"Will you come in? Please. I have my own little room and you will like it."

He could think of nothing he would rather do just then.

"God forgive me, God forgive me!" he said, passion merged with anguish, his words half smothered by a dark wealth of tangled hair.

"He will do, oh He will do!" came with fierce conviction from the girl. Away over the water, he thought, further east but still as always for him so very, very near, a young carpenter on some such evening perhaps may once have known how it was to feel as he felt now. Consoled, the padre allowed himself to be led into the house and the door to be quietly closed behind him.

When on yet another occasion, the same question came to the now rather more experienced padre, the reply was prompt and explosive.

"No, I do not know where The Shop is, and if your wits were about you, you would not ask a priest the way to it."

"Sorry sir, sorry sir," the soldier replied cheerfully. "But if you won't wear a dog-collar it is not easy to see that little badge you wear."

"Dog-collars!" said the padre distastefully. "One of the good things about the army is that I don't often need to wear one."

The man suddenly became very attentive and looked at the padre carefully in the failing light.

"I can't remember that you wore one very often in the village, sir." The padre stared.

"Good heavens!" he said, "Bert Dampier, without a doubt."

Inevitably, their minds returned to a sunny July morning, three years before, when Bert and his Betty had been wed in their west Dorset village, a mile or two from the sea.

"In my last letter from my wife," the padre began cautiously, "she mentioned that Betty's baby was a fine little fellow."

"I don't want to hear about it," came angrily from Bert.

"But you may not know that the boy's father was shot down and killed in a raid on Cologne."

"Well, I won't say it served him right, but it doesn't make any difference to Betty and me."

"She was working at an airfield when she met him; a

tough assignment; heavy air-raids quite often. She is desperately sorry, Bert, and she'd like you back if you will. I wonder if you might adopt that little chap, and let me christen him when we're both back home, and all this is finished with."

"Bloody hell!" said Bert.

But it was noticed that Bert moved away, not further into the town, but back in the direction he had come from, back to his unit.

The padre sighed, a little bubble of happiness rising somewhere inside him. Just for once, he wondered, had he been allowed to be of real use to someone, even if not quite in the heat of battle?

——————— ❧ ———————

Heads
or Tails

Filipino Field-Mouse was a happy young mouse.

He lived with his parents and his brothers and sisters in a fine underground mansion dug in a hedgerow. It had many cosy rooms and storage places, and long twisting corridors that smelt of roots, and made splendid racetracks for Filipino and his friends when his parents were not at home.

Directly facing Mouse Mansion, across the home field, was the Farm House.

To all of them this meant, first and foremost, Thumbo the short-haired Persian lady-cat.

There were other things, of course: clumsy, easily avoided dogs, and even more clumsy children; men and women whom one could often ignore, unless they screamed at you, or because of you; mouse-traps which one learnt to respect at a very early age; food in some quantity, often wrapped up in material which needed a tiresome gnaw or two; the occasional need to clamber up cold wet ivy to an open upper window; and finally, their good cousins the House-Mice, with whom they could stay in winter, and who came to them in the warm weather.

But Thumbo, quiet and graceful and confident, demanded and received their very full attention.

She was the only pussy-cat they had ever seen at close quarters, and they studied her with great care.

Thumbo was a good deal quicker over the ground than they were, but was slow on corners, and her natural cunning was not quite up to their standard.

So they had great fun with her, and "Let's go and tease old Thumbo," was a favourite after-breakfast suggestion from one or another of the younger warrior-mice.

But they all understood very well what a dangerous game they played with pussy, who every so often, elated and tail flying high in triumph, bore off a wriggling morsel between her teeth.

Only two or three of them wore the coveted Tail-Biter's Badge, awarded, sometimes posthumously, to the mouse who successfully nipped Thumbo's tail while she was stalking a fellow mouse, causing an instant change of plan on pussy's part.

On this particular autumn morning, crisp and dewy and fine, cat and mice pursued each other with a gay abandon which all enjoyed.

At the height of the excitement, with the younger mice getting ever more daring, two of them collided head-on a yard from pussy's nose.

One darted away, and the other lay quite still.

Thumbo sailed through the air, landed beside Filipino, and seized him behind an ear.

One or two would-be badge winners made for Thumbo's tail, but she was not to be caught that way on this great occasion.

Head and tail high in the air, she strolled off jauntily towards the Farm House.

Rather fortunately, Filipino was still unconscious. So Thumbo saw no need as yet to administer the usual more or less crippling nip which would reduce any chance of escape while she played cheerfully with her victim.

A little anxiously, she entered the house through the open front door, and glanced into the dining room. A very sleepy dog lay in front of the fire, scratching himself thoughtfully.

She hurried on, hissing and growling ominously in case one or another animal felt inclined to risk a damaged nose or eye.

Looking to left and right, she ran along the passage and into the children's playroom, which was empty. If she could have done so, she would certainly have slammed the door behind her.

Filipino began to regain consciousness as he was dropped gently to the floor, and encouraged with little pats to provide sport for pussy.

He took in the situation at once, and was greatly helped by his knowledge of the room. It was his usual site of entry to the house, through a barred window which was frequently left open at the bottom on fine days.

There was only one mouse-hole in the skirting. He knew it well, as he popped through it regularly in search of his favourite, admired, but somewhat aloof lady cousin Annabel.

It looked rather as if Thumbo knew all about it too, for she placed herself carefully between it and the reviving mouse.

Filipino glanced at the hole, and then at the slight smile on pussy's face; and then hurriedly back with a dawning horror in his eyes.

For Annabel was creeping stealthily from the mouse-hole towards Thumbo's slightly swishing tail.

A moment later, followed by a scream of rage from the agonised pussy-cat, the little mouse sank her pin-sharp teeth deep into the base of Thumbo's tail.

The cat leaped a good three feet into the air, turning towards the mouse-hole as she dropped. Had she jumped a mere two feet, the mice could not possibly have reached the hole ahead of Thumbo's vengeful paws.

But reach it they did, just half a whisker ahead, and pussy's temper was not improved as she listened wrathfully to the happy noises beyond her reach.

It really seemed that Annabel's feelings for Filipino could no longer be described as aloof.

Cuthbert

There's a bit of wall between basin and mirror in our bedroom. On it, one evening, when Mozart's string quartet in D was flowing cheerfully from the radio, a rather small spider swung to and fro on a thread. An arm, a leg, or was it a whisker waved now and then, lightheartedly, one might almost think, conducting the music.

That was two or three weeks ago, and our musical spider is still on the wall, only conducting when his favourite comes on the air, and doubtless composing spider-music at other times, when he is simply known as Cuthbert.

Where basin joins wall, we provide small portions of food. With no flies about, it seems that Cuthbert must be a vegetarian, taking little interest in fish or paté. He will indeed take a cautious sniff at strawberry jam, peanut butter or honey. His firm favourite, however, is whisky marmalade, Cooper's Oxford, of course.

In case a thirsty Cuthbert might fall into the basin, and be faced with a slippery climb comparable to an assault on Mount Everest, flag and all, it seemed reasonable to supply him with a selection of milk bottle tops. These have been filled with assorted contents, and so far milk (pasteurised), water duly filtered, tomato juice and Coca Cola have been provided.

It must be important that Cuthbert has no chance of becoming an alcoholic. But as a modest intake seems now to be considered good for the circulation, a little Hock (Kabinett) has also been offered, and this is varied via the Clarets and the Burgundies until his favourite is found.

For a time it seemed that Cuthbert had little interest in the opposite sex. But one evening, another of his kind came to rest, a leg (or arm) away from Cuthbert, and at dawn next morning they still gazed and gazed at one another. So one wondered if Ben Jonson's unforgettable –

> "Drink to me only with thine eyes,
> And I will pledge with mine,"

– might perhaps be considered relevant.

In any case, Cuthbert's lady love, if such she was, moved briskly away when the morning light disturbed her; and could it be that John Donne's memorable –

> "Busy old fool, unruly Sun, why dost thou thus,
> Through windows, and through curtains call on us?"

– might have satisfied her just then.

But we go on holiday soon, and we worry about Cuthbert.

I wonder if anyone might know of a Spidery, or perhaps a Cattery (4 Star), with a comfortable Annex for small spiders?

───────── ⋰⋱ ─────────

Persian
Pomegranate

There was water in the village, a spring which had failed only once that could be remembered. Its precious product gurgled cheerfully down the only street, and the women washed their clothes and gossiped where the water spread its coolness over crusty rocks. Then it spent itself eagerly among the fruit trees, coaxed and guided here and there along changing channels to quench mounting thirsts.

Several large families dwelt in the village. A handful of mud-brick houses among pomegranate orchards, it lay in a remote valley a dozen miles north of Shiraz, major city of southern Iran. Each family had a narrow strip of orchard running side by side with the others down the valley. Wire fences divided them, and every branch of every tree, perhaps every pomegranate in season, was known and watched with infinite care and devotion. A system of wooden gates guided the water to one or another orchard, and a change of direction was made each evening.

Dominant in her household was Nahid, first wife of Mahmud. Mother of no children, she had decided that not for a moment would she be ignored or displaced for that or any other reason.

"It may be that I shall be barren," she had said sadly to her husband a year or two after marriage. And well before first wives usually contemplate without resentment a rival in the family bed, she had added, "You must have sons for the sheep and the corn, and for the orchard. You can afford a second wife. Is it your wish that I should arrange something for your consideration?"

And after much visiting, much advice from a host of other first wives, and a long talk with the Mullah who had ridden over on his donkey at her special request, she had chosen for him a plump and pretty young woman from the next village. She was one who should satisfy her husband entirely, but who would, Nahid thought, age more readily than herself.

The wedding festivities had lasted a week, and it

was evident that the delighted Mahmud would feed, house and treat his second wife in a manner acceptable to all parties.

The years slipped quickly by, and that willing bearer of useful sons and less useful daughters became entirely absorbed in their upbringing, and in the satisfaction of a demanding husband.

Youngest of her sons was Rashid, sixteen years of age. He, for a year or two, had been responsible for the evening change of flow at the water gates. Quite soon, with the coming of the rains and an abundance of water for every tree, Rashid was to join his brothers to look after the sheep, to help drive them up into the hills at first light, and to bring them down each evening for shelter, for safety from the wolves, and to milk them for the making of cheese, yoghourt and butter.

Recently, Terlan, a girl cousin who was a year or so his junior, had been sent down to help Rashid with the gates, which were difficult to adjust accurately single-handed. A brother might have done this, but she had only elder sisters. At her age, it was not thought quite necessary for Terlan to wear a veil, and during their many happy and playful evening encounters, they would sometimes touch each other seemingly by accident, and then would stop in silent wonder at the strange magic of those occasions.

Meanwhile, Nahid watched warily as her husband and his second wife, both grown portly and a little lazy, slowly tired of each other.

At night, a little bored by lack of variety, Mahmud might allow his mind to dwell on the easy delights of female slave ownership, or perhaps of a month or two of temporary arranged marriage with a widow nearby who had long ago caught his eye. Though both courses were by custom beyond reproach, he knew that either action would please few but himself, and cause un-numbered difficulties with his watchful wives. His second wife, indeed, might even seize such a reasonable opportunity to divorce him and return to her family with the crippling sum he had unwisely agreed to pay her in such an event.

He thought with sudden envy of the head of another family in the village, who was notable because he cheerfully beat his wives at quite regular intervals, and for no apparent reason. It was as though he felt that female discipline in the village should be kept at a reasonable level by this reminder of the accepted authority attached to the practice. Nor, it seemed, did any wife appear to resent it.

Finally, Mahmud turned to his first wife to solve his difficulty for him.

"My brother has many daughters," he told her. "I think he would not grudge me one for my third wife. The Mullah has agreed. Would such a one be acceptable to you, to whom I turn for advice on so many family matters?"

She smiled, and bowed her head to acknowledge the unexpected compliment.

"Your flocks increase, your orchard is mature, you can afford a third wife, and I should welcome a lively young woman to take on some of my duties now. And perhaps I might mention," she added cautiously, "that your second wife and I have spoken of your need for such a change, and she too would welcome a newcomer."

"I will speak to my brother," he replied, much relieved. "His youngest, Terlan I think it is, pleases me."

A shade of alarm passed over Nahid's face. Few things occurred in her family of which she was unaware.

"Perhaps an older one might suit you better."

"Perhaps, and perhaps not," he said, little pleased at this trivial objection to his so reasonable wishes.

That evening Terlan, for the first time, came veiled to the water gates. Both she and Rashid were shy and awkward at this new and unexplored maturity. A farewell to childhood it seemed, for which neither was quite prepared. They said little, and returned early to their homes.

An evening later, they met almost as strangers. Conscious of unknown depths of feeling, they changed the water flow slowly and carefully, spinning out the golden moments which each felt must be their last as friends and playmates.

Finally they faced each other, a step apart, and Rashid gazed spellbound at the pool-deep, so provoking eyes but a pace away. Ripe as any pomegranate, she seemed to him.

"A pest on all veils," he thought, and moved towards her.

Lifting the veil, he kissed her very gently, felt her sudden trembling shudder, heard her quick intake of breath, and watched, bemused, as she turned and fled.

Evenings went by with no Terlan at the gates, and

Rashid felt he had offended, and must be punished.

Then, with clouds in sight at last, the nights cooled and the rains could not be long delayed. So there came an evening when Rashid redirected his bubbling stream for the last time. Listening to the busy, cheerful sound, he sighed and turned for home. As he did so, there was a familiar, longed-for rustle of feet among leaves, and Terlan was by his side, an urgency about her which made him breathless.

"What is it?" he asked.

"You will learn," she replied, "soon enough."

Slowly she removed her veil, dropped it to the ground, and held out her arms in welcome and surrender.

Very early next morning, there came a bellow from the house.

"Where is that infamous son of mine? His first day as shepherd, his flock of sheep should be half way up the hills by now, and there is no sign of him."

Mahmud's first wife started to soothe him when an angry figure appeared at the door.

"Where is that infernal daughter of mine?" came from an enraged brother, who cast suspicious looks at Mahmud. "You are not married to her yet."

"Fool!" was the reply.

They stared at each other for a few moments, the same unwelcome thought slowly coming to both.

"The water gates," they said in unison.

Hastening down, the two approached the tree-sheltered gates cautiously, and stopped speechless as they reached them.

Deeply asleep, close in each other's arms, lay the son of one, and the daughter of the other.

With a growl of fury, Mahmud put his hand to his curved and jewelled dagger, and moved towards the couple.

His brother, not quite sure who the victim was to be, laid a firm hand on his arm.

"Let them sleep," he said. "I have other daughters who will please you no less."

That evening, Mahmud was unusually quiet, and his wives raised no topic for conversation.

"I have thought," he said at last, "and maybe you are right. My brother's eldest daughter is more buxom, and carries herself well, and would understand a man's needs better. Would you be agreeable to her joining the family?"

"Of course," was the quiet reply. "Of course."

Dog's Delight

"Let's take a turn on the beach," said my wife. "There's not much wind, the tide is out, and there's just a touch of sun, now and again."

I looked cautiously through the window facing south-west, and saw the long thin bar of rock looking quite like a surfacing submarine with its shallow prominence amidships. This told us that the tide was just right for a walk on rich, firm sand which might be a trifle moist, but not yet powdery.

As usual, Rupert the dog jumped up on a chair to share our inspection of the coast. He may have drawn similar conclusions about the sand and its suitability for walking, but probably he simply wished to make sure the sea was still there, and waiting for him.

He was fairly easy to cope with on the beach. An

infinite friendliness towards almost all living creatures, combined with an indisputable mastery in the art of tail-wagging for all occasions, made social life easy for him.

Pools were his seashore speciality, and his love-hate relationship with crabs was the light and pride of his life.

His technique was both simple and dangerous. As long as a crab was mostly under water, the dog was superior in battle. The beastie's claws moved less quickly through the water than a dog's jaws, and Rupert could grasp its back lightly and fling it through the air with that special doggy yelp of joy only to be heard by the sunny seaside. Once on the sand, the dog treated the crab with marked respect. Rupert valued his lips and nose, and his snaps were prudent and always carefully out of range.

But today was just a little different. Spring was in the air, crocuses had burst upon the scene, and what could a good dog do but greet it with a show of bravado suitable for the occasion.

Rupert duly found his crab, a splendid creature with watchful jet-black eyes on sturdy stalks, a bounteous waist, and dainty painted finger nails, or equivalent female crustacean weaponry.

From deep in her pool the slow-moving crab was hoisted on high and flicked across the sand, where she quickly gathered her wits together, and faced her enemy.

Rupert did his usual lap of honour, romping round his booty and waving his tail to his appreciative supporters.

Suddenly casting caution and experience to forgotten winter winds, he moved in and snapped at his opponent's gleaming eyes.

At once there was a yelp of despair, a tail was lowered like a flag at sunset, and a despondent dog presented himself to me with crab firmly attached to his nose.

Town bred, and knowing little of such matters, I turned to my wife for help and instruction. She was some distance away and seemed just then to be busy hunting for something deep in a bag; but I felt sure, or almost sure, that the lift at the corners of her mouth could not possibly be a hastily banished smile.

I must tackle this myself, I felt, and grabbed, I thought and hoped, the shell of the crab. But the beastly thing got there first, and the next I knew was that one of my fingers was painfully and irretrievably gripped by one nipper, and that Rupert's nose was as firmly held by the other.

I hastily seized the dog under my free arm, and again turned to my wife for aid and sympathy.

"What am I to do?" I bleated helplessly, and could not now fail to notice the suppressed giggle, speedily altered to an unconvincing cough.

"Dr. Adam has his surgery just now," she said. "Perhaps he might help. That or the Fire Brigade."

I believe that neither Rupert nor myself will recall with much pleasure the walk back to the car. It was a nice morning, and friends of both of us, human and doggy, showed much interest in our dilemma, and dealt out suggestions in profusion.

The surgery, of course, was crowded, but our predicament allowed instant access to our good doctor.

His hearty bellow of laughter we thought unnecessary, but he lost little time.

"We've some chloroform somewhere, I think," he said to the nurse.

Laying a pad of gauze over the glassy black eyes, he soaked it with the drug, and watched our relief as the nippers relaxed, and he gave gentle succour to a very sore nose, and a very sore finger.

"Queen Victoria had the stuff for her last two confinements," he told us. "She was pleased with it too."

Coffee
with Liz

My first visit to Liz Peters' café occurred about noon, and I asked for a coffee. The place was empty, and the tables laid for lunch. The pretty young waitress seemed to have doubts at first as to whether she should accept my order, but soon relented.

Through the archway was the kitchen, brightly lit. Bustling to and fro was a little woman in her mid-thirties. She had the determined look and quick movements of someone who had needed to make decisions at short notice all her life.

As I waited, the door opened and a young man, leather-jacketed, came in without haste and asked for cigarettes. The girl opened her mouth to reply, but the woman was a word or two ahead of her.

"No, no cigarettes," she said firmly. "And why is it," she went on, "that when anyone comes and asks for cigarettes they always have to leave the door open?" It was indeed a rather cold day.

"O.K., Gran'ma," the youngster replied irreverently, "keep your hair on! That is, of course, if it's your own!" And with this well-worn witticism he marched out cheerfully, leaving the door open.

The next entrant was quite different. She came in, her scarlet and green sari making little silky noises as she moved, and looking like some wayward orchid that had strayed from a heated greenhouse. Her features were moulded with much delicacy, and she walked with an economy of gesture that was both feminine and graceful.

"I wonder," she said very distinctly, "if you would allow me to use your telephone for a very short call," and she proffered a £1 coin.

Liz, hands on hips and head a little forward, had her decks cleared for action and was fully prepared to attack. But she wrestled visibly and at some length with the teasing problem of whether or not to open up with her considerable armament against this seemingly vulnerable foe, so palpably clad in the ancient defences of grace and beauty.

Finally, Liz Peters' hands slid to her sides, her

expression softened, and she walked slowly to the door, closed it, and walked back.

"All right, love, it's through that door. But I'll tell you this, it's a good job you're not staying for lunch, for it'll be bloody well ruined today." But Liz did cautiously allow herself to be charmed by the little wordless bow she received from her visitor.

When the door opened again, a tall bearded man of about forty-five strolled in with leisurely bearing, closed the door carefully, and looked about him.

Liz Peters was barely in sight, intent on cooking, but no degree of culinary concentration could have withstood the "Liz!" from the stranger, which seemed to set the cutlery a-chattering and the plates a-dance.

"Ben!" came from the kitchen, and Liz shot by and literally sailed through the last yard or two into waiting arms.

It was an embrace on a grand scale, and when completed to the satisfaction of both, they sank relieved into the nearest chairs.

"What happened, Ben?" she asked after a pause.

"Well, I suppose it must be nearly two years," he said slowly.

"Two years last Thursday," she corrected, and he rewarded her with a look of amused respect.

"As you know well," he went on, "I needed to leave the country in rather a hurry."

"I know it well enough," replied Liz, "just twenty-eight days before we were to be married."

"I went to South America," Ben went on. "Set up in business there. I've done quite well. Come over now to expand a bit."

Liz leant back and her eyes had a soft and starry glow which perhaps had not been kindled there since she was a child.

"I think I should like that, Ben," she said in a low voice.

"I could set up a café, couldn't I? The beef would be cheap anyway," and she laughed contentedly.

"Liz," Ben spoke in a husky voice, "I got myself married in South America. We've a kid."

Liz was quite used to the frequent need for quick adjustment. But on this occasion she felt herself almost overwhelmed, and the sympathetic seconds passed slowly by with shaded eyes as she strove with the blessing of Ben's embrace, enticing visions of South America, and now with the brutal barrier of a dark-eyed supplanter and her child.

"Bother!" she said at last, and the unexpected word danced lightly round the room, and only gently came to rest. But tension was relieved, and time sped unhindered on its way once again.

"Well, I'll be damned!" came from Ben with a makeshift grin of disbelief.

Liz had always regarded the quiet little word she had used as the most desirable understatement in the language. Until now, it had remained unattainable, a wistful possibility, just out of reach, and always thrust aside in moments of stress by cruder material.

With a sigh of resigned understanding it came to her that, defeated in her battle for Ben, she had at least achieved something, and might achieve just a little something more.

She reached for a menu, and on its back wrote

CIGARETTES SOLD FROM NEXT TUESDAY
PAYPHONE AVAILABLE SHORTLY

She got up and placed it prominently in the window. Then, ignoring Ben, she turned towards her kitchen.

Not altogether dissatisfied with her day's work so far, Liz was soon deeply and audibly concerned in a series of rescue operations among her pots and her pans.

—————— ✺ ——————

Name
and Number

A house built on stilts has certain advantages over others. It is pleasantly provoking, with visions of fishing from balconies, of rising waters, and of rescues from house-tops; and perhaps of safety from reptiles and other invaders.

There are few uncontrolled floods and not very many dangerous reptiles nowadays in a North Queensland city. But some of the houses continue to be built on stilts. It is said to be cooler that way.

There was one such house, with fine cast-iron metalwork softening the angles, and with latticed woodwork about its windows. It looked out, from the lower slopes of the hill, to a group of tree-clad coral islands.

A child sat on the lowest step of the stairway leading to the balcony, and cried bitterly. Once or twice he looked at his father, sitting nearby, and the look of reproach on the boy's face was to haunt Andrew from time to time for the rest of his days.

"You could have saved her, dad."

"Not really, son. There was a whole family of the bastards lashing about within a few yards of her. They'd have torn me to shreds before I got anywhere near. She didn't want us both to die.

He walked slowly down the garden. She had planned and he had planted it nearly ten years ago, and by now a casual wealth of colour could both bewilder and enchant. Unable to share its riches with his Anne, he barely noticed the abundance of blue-flowered Thunbergia, of rose-crimson Bougainvillea, of scarlet-leaved Poinsettia and whitest Frangipani; it was of little concern to him that there were trees heavy with seed, Jacarandas and Poincianas, to remind one that other seasons would provide no less lovely flowers.

He had been down in the cabin of his little yacht, looking at a catalogue with Bobby, when the cry had reached them.

Up on deck in a moment, he saw that Anne was twenty yards from the yacht, and that two pairs of sliver-grey fins and their potent owners were circling their victim and edging nearer. Other pairs, further away, seemed to be taking an interest, and awaiting an outcome.

Andrew grabbed a life-belt and hurled it into the sea, hoping that it might distract the sharks' attention.

Anne was making for the yacht at her best speed, and would pass the life-belt on her way. The sea was calm, with scarcely a ruffle to interfere with her rhythmic and relaxed arm movements. Hope grew slowly as Andrew watched those strong young shoulders urge her through the water, and approved the little ripple astern as her feet just broke the surface. Anne, swimming for her life, was obeying all the rules, and needed only good fortune to bring her to safety.

But as she passed the belt she hesitated, lifted her head and screamed, went under for a moment, and reappeared by the belt. She grasped it and slipped into its circle, resting her arms on its red covering.

"The axe, quick!" and Bobby grabbed it from its hook in the hatchway, and handed it to his father.

The position in all its grim reality seemed crystal-clear to Andrew, and he knew just what he must do.

He grasped the slim railing prior to vaulting into the sea, and quickly glanced at Anne to judge his distance from her. She was gazing at him calmly, and to his consternation and wonder there was in her eyes a look of finality and grief, something beyond dispute or rejection that till then had felt no need to surface in all their time together. With it came a little shake of the head, and her message was firm and absolute, and froze his fingers to the rail before his feet could leave the deck.

A few moments later the look on Anne's face changed to one of agony, and she disappeared from his sight, leaving a life-belt bobbing gently in the sea, and distantly on the hillside, a house on stilts, clean and white and friendly.

He walked on down the garden, wondering why he had obeyed her. He had little doubt of his own fate had he entered the water, but his intention to do so had been fixed and indisputable. Only Anne could have changed it, and that she had done with but a look and a gesture. Fear, at that moment of hesitation when Anne chose sacrifice rather than a possibility of rescue, first had a chance to invade his mind. Had it helped to change it? He knew that Bobby thought so, and perhaps would not readily forgive him. He felt he might never be quite sure himself. And as he walked on slowly to the pool at the end of the garden, Andrew remembered that a mile away, the other side of the hill, were the headstones of hundreds of his young countrymen, killed in war and brought back here to lie in their own land. In just so many hundreds of unknown, unremembered ways they each had faced, and, willingly or unwillingly, accepted their ends. The knowledge of how they died, well or less well, proud or ashamed, died with them. For most, no record but a headstone, with name and number. His own father had been one of them. Of his much-loved Anne, brown-haired, brown-eyed, brown-bodied, cheerful about the mouth and eyes, loyal and devoted beyond measure, he knew he could be proud. Perhaps at the end she had felt just a moment of pride herself. He wished just then – how sincerely he was not quite sure – that she had allowed him to share that with her.

He felt a small paw pushed into his hand, and gave it a squeeze.

"You know, Bobby," he said, "I believe we should keep this garden just as it is." A sort of headstone, he added to himself; no name, no number. The paw gave a tug, half agreement, half entreaty.

"Can I do the weeding?"

Andrew laughed. He had forgotten the child's simple delight which had so pleased and surprised them, turning into a privilege what was a punishment for most little boys.

"My word, you can!"

He knelt on the grass to give his son a hug as he and Anne, one after the other to satisfy Bobby's love of order, had so often done.

"Only one hug now, I'm afraid."

The boy nodded his head, and buried it in his father's arms.

—————— ❦ ——————

Toes
in the Sea

Tito had little on his beautifully proportioned sixteen-year-old body.

A strip of colour round his loins and that was all.

Just now, very alert and observant, he walked along the beach just where sand and sea meet. It always pleased him to be there.

In a flash he could forget his rather difficult world and be twisting and turning in the warm caresses of the water or floating idly in the lazy waves of this tideless sea.

He resisted the temptation for he had important business in hand.

As casually as possible he was watching a middle-aged couple leaving the hotel. This was built on rocks rising twenty feet above a fine stretch of near-white sand.

They came down slowly in the heat, dropped their towels and a handbag and went on to bathe.

Tito circled slowly to give the couple time to swim away, and approached the little heap of belongings. As he did so, a girl, evidently intent on joining her parents, raced across the sand from the hotel and arrived breathless at the towels at almost exactly the same moment as did Tito.

After the first shock of surprise they gazed calmly at each other, both suddenly and for the first time in their lives, completely aware of their own and of another's beauty, and both unwilling to terminate this long appraisal before it was quite necessary.

But something had to be said, though she doubted if he would understand more than a word or two.

She was not to know that his grandfather, who had lived with the boy's family for the last ten years, had spent the previous thirty in America; and that he had insisted on passing on to his reluctant grandchildren what he knew of the language and some of what he knew of the art world in which he had worked.

"I saw you last week in Florence," she said casually in English, "but in marble, or was it bronze, and by your Donatello, I think. But you look much better as you are. Why can't all statues come to life, or at least the lovely ones," and she thought of some she preferred should stay in stone.

"One or other of the 'Davids' perhaps," replied Tito absently, "there is one in each material." The conversation did not interest him.

"If you had not arrived just then I should by now be out of sight with your mother's handbag." Tito could not hide his irritation.

"I am so sorry, I can be so tactless. You know," she went on, "I doubt if I could stop you if you just carried on with your plan."

"No," he replied, stung by her suggestion of complicity, "it would not do now, and my family must find the money some other way."

"I don't suppose there is a thing worth having anyway; let's see," and she opened the handbag and tumbled out its contents slowly on to the sand.

Among the expected feminine bric-a-brac was a half-open lipstick, beginning to melt, which became studded with sand-grains, and they laughed together at its patent loss of further function; then a small and elegant gold wrist watch, a twin-jewelled engagement ring whose fine stones nestled incongruously among their fellows in the sand, and an exquisite Louis Quinze scimitar brooch.

"Mum's done it again," said the girl with a sigh.

"She sheds her jewels before a bathe, meaning to lock them in her suitcase. Then puts them in her handbag instead. Quite a good haul," she went on and looked at him questioningly. But his gaze had moved away and his thoughts were elsewhere.

"One day," he said to the sea very quietly in Italian, "I should like to marry this girl."

But not quietly enough.

"I'm sure that would be very nice," he heard her say politely in the same language, and looking back at the girl he saw her blue eyes darken and sparkle.

There was a long moment which, with the few others of similar intensity that are the ration of most mortals, was to be treasured by them both.

"Come," and she grasped his hand and they raced to the yielding sea and scattered their emotions among bubbles and seaweed and laughter.

The family did not return to the resort for several years. When they did, Tito was a waiter at the hotel with a maturing masculine beauty and a natural dignity which caused many a female eye to rest willingly upon him.

The two said no word, but on one occasion looked long and carefully at one another, filling in the years between.

When she came again it was with her husband and two children. Tito was by then manager, and under his serene guidance the hotel dealt lovingly and efficiently with its changing cargoes so that few left at the end of their spell without a sigh of regret.

The two children, as though by instinctive right, at once adopted the splendid Tito, appointed him their swimming coach in his spare moments, and regarded him as their joint holiday godfather.

The visits and the years went by until at length she came alone, her children married and her husband dead.

The third time this happened, when Tito had become owner of the hotel and foreshore, was just forty years after a portion of sand had ruined an unregretted length of lipstick.

He wondered if some significance might be read into such a span.

As always, he carried tea to her at a well remembered spot on the beach where he had set her shade and chair.

It is possible that on this day his hand shook as he handed it to her.

It is certain that on to the long-suffering sand his tray shed sugar, saucer and cup, milk and milkjug, and a chocolate cake, beginning to melt, which became closely studded with sand-grains.

And, as once before, they laughed together at its sad loss of further usefulness.

"Come," she said, jumping up and taking Tito's hand, and with eyes willing and still young enough to darken and sparkle, "we have been busy, you and I, and can no longer run like the wind, nor are we quite suitably dressed for bathing. But at least," and she laughed gaily at their fallen status, "we can paddle."

And on his way Tito repeated his message to the inattentive sea. "One day," he said, no more and no less quietly than on another occasion, "I should like to marry this girl."

Golden
Foxes

At last, in reply to her rapidly diminishing cry of "Danishga, Danishga!" a taxi relented and took Helena in. She was surprised to find one passenger only. More often, there would be four or five picked up at random, and filling every inch. Such was the crowded, excitable city of Shiraz, in the later days of the Shah of Persia.

In the back sat an elegantly dressed woman, sobbing, Helena thought, as she might have done had she been the last survivor in a shattered world.

It is difficult to remain inactive for long in close company with grief of this quality.

After a spell Helena, a quiet, dark, gentle girl whose movements tended to be graceful and sufficient, took the woman's right hand in both of hers, patted it firmly, and made noises which she hoped were internationally consoling.

The sobbing stopped at once, and they stared at

GOLDEN FOXES

each other. Helena saw a face still startlingly beautiful, not now young, not quite yet resigned to a life where love was no longer a priority.

The lady wiped her eyes slowly, wearing only for a moment the anxious look of all women who have been unwise enough to weep.

"I heard your destination," she said in English with a refreshing hint of some French connection long ago. "I live very near. Please to come in and take tea. It would give much pleasure."

There could be no refusing such an invitation, given with an unexpected blend of charm and authority.

The familiar frustration of high-walled gardens quickly turned to pleasure as the dullest of doors in the dullest of streets was unlocked, and Helena followed her hostess into the colourful private world beyond; the fountained pool, the trellised vine, pomegranate, peach and peony, roses and sunlight. Always sunlight, eleven months in any twelve.

They sat on swinging garden seats in shade by the pool, drinking tea and looking up at the almost theatrically barren and lifeless hills which lie round much of the town.

"My husband," said the lady at length, with an eloquent spread of hands, "he has just died in hospital after a traffic accident."

"I understand. I am so sorry."

"I think I am sorry too. I do not know yet. I have cried, and perhaps that will be enough."

Helena felt there was little she could contribute just then, and waited.

"You are a stranger, and a kind one. So you will, I think, forgive me if I unburden my mind a little."

"Of course, of course!"

After two years of teaching in one of the Departments of Pahlavi University, by good fortune

English-speaking to some extent, she found herself surprised and even irritated to be termed a stranger. She had quickly come to love this astonishing city, and the explosive language which she felt she could at last begin to handle. And most of all she had come to love her own devoted citizen, as lively as his city, his hair greying just a very little at beard-tip and temple.

"My husband's family," the lady was saying, "have been important dealers in carpets in the city for generations. But his hobby was always the treasure at Persepolis, and what became of it. In recent years we would go there often, and spend many happy hours exploring the ruins, and the hills above and the plains below them."

"But surely," Helena asked, "the story is that Alexander and his army sacked and burnt the palace, and made off with the treasure on innumerable camels, oxen, horses and anything else available on two or four legs?"

"Yes, yes, indeed! and almost certainly true up to a point."

"How so?"

"The Persian Emperors built themselves this splendid palace, and into the great treasury went most of the

95

tribute and gifts showered on them from far and wide. But my husband believed that the best of those gifts, the loveliest things from east and west, were trusted to no treasury when Alexander was marching steadily east, and defeating every army that could be raised against him. And who can blame Alexander if he burnt the place down in sheer fury at finding so little treasure to his liking."

Helena laughed ruefully. "And what became of the best of the treasure?"

"Ah, the best! Those exquisite things would be given to one or two Zoroastrian priests for safe keeping in their temples. Any loss or damage could mean death to those priests, so they would surely keep them buried deep in the foundations of their great fire-temples."

"But that was over two thousand years ago," objected Helena. "Surely your country has been knocked about by two or three quite different empires since Alexander's time. There's the Seleucids, and the Sassonians, and finally of course the Arabs in six or seven hundred A.D. Would not one or another of them, during those thousands of years have reduced your temples to dust?"

"No, no, no! Not at all, not at all! If changes came, religious leaders would be only too glad to find a sacred building ready and waiting for them. They would alter it to suit themselves, as others will have done before them, and add a dome or two and a minaret. But you know something of our history?"

"A little, from a friendly countryman of yours, mostly."

"Well, no doubt over the centuries many of the treasures will have been sold or stolen. But not long ago, a Mullah who was a personal friend offered my husband what the Mullah thought might be one of the last of the treasures. This was in exchange for many rare and beautiful carpets to cover the great floors of his mosque. My husband did not hesitate."

They were quiet for a while, and Helena thought with pleasure of the little collection of ancient work in her own apartment, given her by her so very close friend, and purchased, as he had carefully explained to her, from Arab tribesmen who dug them up in desert sites known only to themselves.

"It was a shallow bowl of gold," the lady continued, "six-sided, and worked with much delicacy. It was borne, at alternate angles, on the backs of three fine young galloping foxes. A fourth fox, perhaps their mother, sat in the bowl achieving affectionate unconcern with some difficulty as they raced around in never-ceasing circles."

Helena had no word to say, and there was a pause.

"But we quarrelled about its fate. My husband wished to keep it. Impossible! I loved it as much as he, but I would not have it in the house for more than a few days. It must go of course to the museum at Teheran to join the pitifully few treasures from Persepolis which they have there. But he took it away, and we drifted apart from that time. I believe he found feminine refreshment elsewhere, and perhaps a home for the foxes."

The lady's face showed sudden concern.

"My dear, are you quite well?" For Helena had closed her eyes, and lowered her forehead on to her right hand.

"Yes, but will you forgive me if I leave you for a few minutes," and she stood up, held the back of her seat for a moment to steady herself, and quickly left the house.

On her return, she placed before the lady a large rounded object wrapped in silk, which she very carefully removed.

"You will know best what should be done with this."

"So," said the lady after a long, long pause, and Helena noticed with a little warm feeling of relief that her eyes were not unkind.

"It is you who have lost a lover, and I who am bereft of but a husband. The world, I am afraid, will give you no sympathy, and will give me too much."

They gazed at one another for a few moments, too sadly thoughtful for further speech.

Then their eyes turned to the four foxes and their mood lightened, as would that of many another lucky enough to look upon them in years to come.

Helena stooped, kissed the lady very gently, and moved away across the garden, past fountained pool and trellised vine, pomegranate, peach and peony, slowly through the sunlight to the gate in the whitened wall.

Come
Tuesday

Once or twice during his four or five years as a student, Jeremy had seen a girl, in the street, at a party, talking to someone else on the underground, and thought "That one would do, I could marry that lovely girl." But the years ahead had to be filled with much work, and a little play; and beauty, tug as it might, had been allowed to slip by with only a glance of admiration, an experience familiar to every young man that ever roamed the streets.

But one day this early spring, Jeremy was walking briskly over Putney Bridge, and raised his eyes from the river as he became aware of footsteps whose liveliness could only be feminine.

She was not looking at him, but what fascinated him was not her good looks which seemed entirely satisfactory, but the friendly amusement which danced and sparkled in the very deepest of blue eyes, which he felt sure had only just glanced away from his own. Of course, he was all too well aware of a dozen reasons that might have caused that smile; the lovely spring morning with the hint of buds on every tree; the two little dogs approaching each other with cautious interest across the road; the man of her choice she was perhaps to meet a few hundred yards up Putney Hill. But he had to find out.

So after a few steps he came to a halt, hesitated, turned, and still dazzled by those eyes, followed the girl along Putney High Street. She turned in at the Post Office, and he watched her through a window as she bought a stamp and posted a letter. As she left the building they were face to face, and he did not step aside.

"May I speak to you?" he asked, and noticed with foreboding that the eyes no longer danced or sparkled.

It was a relief to him just then that they were urged politely aside and out of the way.

"If I were an artist," he went on hastily, "it would be easier. I should tell you that I passed you on the bridge, that you were almost exactly right for a portrait I was about to do of Madonna and Child for the new window in St. Cuthbert's church across the river, though cheek bones just a trifle higher, and eyes just a little further apart, might have suited . . ."

"And I suppose," she interrupted with light sarcasm, "you'd have suggested you might ask my parents for permission for me to sit for you?" She edged very slightly towards the busy passers by.

"I doubt it. I should have hoped you would be so pleased with the thought of appearing in an East window for the next five hundred years or so, that reluctance would have been unthinkable."

"I seem to remember," the girl replied coldly, but warming unwillingly to the subject, "that four or five centuries ago, a certain Fra Filippo Lippi persuaded a young Florentine nun to sit for his Madonna and Child. The consequences, I believe, were not entirely happy ones."

Jeremy had spent more than one exhausting holiday toiling up the hills of central Italy on a bicycle to visit the hilltop and other cities of that area, and fill his mind with unforgettable buildings, and pictures, and frescoes.

"Filippo Lippi," he said, surprised and delighted to have come across a subject which interested her, "found himself the loveliest girl in all of Tuscany, and five hundred years later you'll find her looking just as lovely in one or another gallery or church in Florence or Prato or wherever. They simply fell in love, and what was the result but another famous painter, Filippino Lippi, perhaps a finer artist than his father."

"Possibly. But you seem to have forgotten that Filippo Lippi was one of the most notorious libertines of his day, that he refused to marry his Lucrezia in spite of having the Pope's permission and encouragement, and that he was finally poisoned by the relatives of his last mistress, at the tender age of sixty-three."

"Yes, yes," said Jeremy, gathering what strength was left to him. "But he also seems to have been one of the best-liked men of his time. His many sins were widely forgiven him because of his charm and generosity, and Lucrezia never left him from the day of her seduction to the day of his death. They may even have been very happy together."

The subject exhausted, there was a moment's silence. The girl looked around, and seemed about to depart.

"Give me only the smallest of hints," he urged. "I'm sure you won't tell me who you are, but I'll find out if you'll let me have no more than the scent on a very small handkerchief to work on."

The suspicion of a smile lit up the ice-cold eyes, and was hastily banished. An anxious young man watched as his fate was decided for him.

"This paper-back," she said after some moments of hesitation, "was written by a friend of mine. I meant to post it back to him today in a suitable envelope. But I found I was short of money when I tried to buy one. Find him if you can, return it to him, and he may or may not be willing to help you."

And she was gone.

Bewildered, Jeremy walked down to the river, sat on a bench and looked at the book.

The Fossil-bearing Cliffs of Dorset, by Andrew Dunn, he read on the lively cover. It was not, for him, an inspiring subject, and he let a few sunny days pass before he set about his task.

The telephone books proved unhelpful, and a brief skirmish with a stony-voiced employee at directory enquiries confirmed that the number was ex-directory. And after a very few words with the publishers, he was advised that a letter from the caller would be duly forwarded to the author, should the caller so wish.

The caller decided that he did so wish, and a cautious note praised Andrew Dunn for his fine book, and asked for an interview. An absence of reply then gave Jeremy a chance to read the book, and a little time was spent recovering from that ordeal.

He had noticed from the title page that Dunn was a lecturer at London University. Geology Department it must be, and a request there for information about senior personnel provided Jeremy with a lady helper. But a suggestion of lifelong friendship with the author, some mountain-climbing together as students, and an assurance that only a couple of days remained of his holiday from distant lands, were needed to provide a telephone number.

Things then moved along briskly.

"I've a book of yours to return to you," he told the author on the phone. "It's inscribed to Pauline, and the young lady asked me to let you have it back."

"Did she say why?"

"No, I don't think she did. Perhaps it's not quite her subject."

"Could you bring it to my rooms?" and he gave an address in a University building.

Jeremy wasted no time, and a little later he handed the book over, and was glad to be rid of it.

"Have you known Pauline long?" Andrew asked.

"No, can't say I have."

Andrew glanced at his watch.

"Time I stopped work. Let's go uninvited and find out what's on her mind. She'll be working in her garden this fine evening, and may be better-tempered with a third person present."

As they drove through the London streets, Andrew seemed glad to talk.

"This young woman, Pauline Ross, is a sound commercial artist, and a very good illustrator. She does what she's told to do, does it well, and does not argue," he told Jeremy. "She did the illustrations for this book, and I hoped she would do those for my next one. But we quarrelled about other things, and I've not been allowed to visit or even talk to her for months."

They passed over Putney Bridge and, turning right into one of the little streets near the river, stopped before a white cottage, bow-windowed, semi-detached, and somewhat dominated by a large brass knocker on the front door.

Andrew had no doubts about procedure. The knocker was allowed to drop with thunderous results and, seeming not to expect any response, Andrew walked round the house and through a gate to a little walled garden at the back.

Pauline, looking ravishing Jeremy thought, in suitably casual clothes, rose from a garden chair, put aside a drawing board, and greeted them politely, with neutral eyes. And an assumption by Andrew that a kiss would be acceptable, received no encouragement.

"I wondered if you'd given up," she said to Jeremy. "I felt you might have one or two little difficulties, or was it . . ."

"Why did you send the book at all," interrupted Andrew, "it was a gift to you. And why . . ?"

"Do be quiet," said Pauline severely, "just sit down and relax, and I'll give you both a drink."

A little later, comfortable and attentive, the two men waited for whatever might come.

"Now," she said, "I gave your book to this young man on the spur of the moment, a quite silly thing to do I've no doubt. It was simply because he amused and pleased me with his absurd picture of himself girl-hunting with nothing to help him but a very small handkerchief with a drop or two of perfume. I sent the book back to you to make sure you understood things were ended between us, socially, work-wise, and in every other way."

"Then you won't illustrate my new book?"

"Thank you, but I'd rather not."

"But why, why, why?" asked Andrew angrily.

It seemed that nothing but the truth would suffice.

"Mainly because you are altogether too bossy to work for in comfort. You gave me no peace, and allowed me no part in any decision except design of the cover. I'd rather be out of work than bullied by you or anybody else, and I'm not out of work. Your needs were quite easily provided, but any ideas of my own were promptly sat on, and pushed firmly out of sight."

"And what did you expect? You are no geologist, and know nothing of fossils. You were not a particularly experienced artist at the time, and were lucky to get the job."

"What I do know," she replied, "is that any subject can be presented with imagination and perhaps with charm, and that you allowed neither of these to surface at any point in your prose or in my illustrations. To most readers, your books will always be infinitely dull, and working with you more or less intolerable."

Andrew rose with fury in his eyes, and made for the gate.

Suddenly remembering Jeremy, he turned.

"Will you come?" he asked.

"Not if I am allowed to stay."

Both men looked at the girl, who gave no sign, and Jeremy was left to his fate.

Peace crept slowly back into the garden, warily at first, and then with confidence.

"I believe," said Jeremy very quietly, "that, a corner or two away, there's an Italian restaurant with considerable pizza skills. Do you think we might explore what progress may have been made with those skills?"

Pauline allowed herself just a moment of hesitation.

"Thank you, but not tonight. I've work to do."

"Next week, perhaps?"

"Pizza's on Tuesdays usually, though I can't think why." And she walked into her cottage and closed the door, leaving Jeremy alone in her garden, hopeful and by no means unhappy.

Weaker Sex

"Hop in!" the man had said without asking their destination, and since it was raining and cars were scarce, they had thought it best to scramble in without further conversation.

Mark, owner of a pair of mischievous twinkling eyes which lightened his over-rugged features, threw their haversacks into the back seat and climbed in beside them.

Helen, black-haired, deep blue-eyed, vivid in her red windcheater, got in by the driver.

"Thanks for stopping," Mark said, "we're hoping to get to Lyme Regis by tonight."

"How important is that for you?"

"Not vital, but we're expected."

"Would there be anxiety if you arrived late?"

"Disappointment, I like to think. But why?"

Mark and Helen, who had hoped for a peaceful and

relaxed spell in the comfortable Rover Vitesse, were suddenly very alert indeed. There was a tenseness and excitement in the man's voice, and they seemed to be travelling rather fast.

"When I picked you up I thought you were both men. My apologies. I can be very unobservant," and he turned a brief but decidedly charming smile towards Helen on his left.

"If you had known," she asked, "would you have left us in the rain?"

"Yes."

There was the sound of laughter from the back seat.

"You could just drop us off again, you know. We're quite good walkers, even in the rain."

"Barely afford the time. Do you see that car ahead. It's a Ford Granada and I'm tailing it. The driver is doing his best to shake me off. I nearly lost him when I stopped for you."

They waited anxiously for further enlightenment.

"I was doing a little peaceful shopping in Kingston when I walked into a bank hold-up. Two armed men got away with what looked like a good haul. My car was handy, so I followed them," and he glanced not unhappily at the speedometer as it hovered near the hundred mark.

"Will you stay with me?" he asked. "Of course I must stop if you'd rather not. I wanted some youthful support, but it's quite different with a girl as part of it. My name's Tom Avery, by the way."

The two youngsters looked at each other a little blankly.

This was an important weekend for them.

In two months Mark was to go abroad, probably for several years. If they were to marry, it must be decided very soon. Mark knew what he wanted. Helen needed a nudge from somewhere, in one or the other direction. Perhaps in some way related to this need, she nodded her head very slightly.

"We'll stay," said Mark, and there was silence in the car for a while.

"I know this area well," Mark continued. "There's a turning left in about a mile. It's a sort of bypass. If you take it, and they don't, they'll have to go through the village you can see; road mending goes on there, with at least one traffic stop. That and a heap of twisty turnings should slow them down. We'd rejoin the main road some distance beyond the village, and I'd guess we would be about a minute ahead."

"What then?"

"We turn back towards the village for a few yards, then swing the car across the road to block half of it. They'll think we hit a car that didn't stop. Helen moves across and slumps over the wheel. You and I hop out and lie across the road, very unconscious indeed. You avoid letting them see your face."

"And what's to follow?"

"I reckon they'll pull up, jump out and haul us off the road. That's when we go for them. You need two hands to haul fourteen stone of man, and I doubt if they could clutch a weapon as well."

"I don't think I've lost much since I last weighed myself," and Tom patted his tum contentedly. "I was over fifteen then."

"What if they don't stop?" asked Helen quietly.

"Too bad. But I think they will. We shall look like a range of mini-mountains."

Helen shuddered, as Tom slowed and turned left.

As they thudded down the lesser road she thought with longing of the cottage near the Cobb where they hoped to stay the night; and of their walk along the Lyme Bay beach tomorrow to Charmouth, hunting for fossils tucked all too tidily in their bed of blue lias.

The car slowed again at the next junction, turned back towards the village, and halted half across the road, well short of a bend in the main road.

They were only just in their agreed positions when a car with anger in its heart swayed round the bend, and

came to a reluctant and noisy halt with a yard or two to spare.

Two men jumped out, the older holding an automatic.

"Quick, off the road with them. Our friend won't be far behind," and the younger one set to work.

"Blast and damn!" said Helen quietly in the Rover. That automatic. They had gambled on both men doing the body moving at the same time.

Unable to raise a protesting finger, Mark was pulled into the ditch beside the road, and Tom was beginning to slide in the same direction.

Helen meanwhile noticed that Tom had left the gears in neutral, and, in his hurry, had left the hand-brake off.

The man with the gun was standing a yard from the Rover and taking little notice of her.

Suddenly, she realised she had a weapon, and a potent one.

Did she dare to use it, she wondered, her heart racing painfully.

She was a skilled driver and saw no difficulties.

In a moment the car was started, a gear engaged, and they were lurching violently forward, collecting the man untidily on the bumper and radiator, and hurling him into the ditch where he lay very still.

With a shout of delight, Mark leapt into action, dealt neatly and expertly with the man who was having difficulty pulling Tom off the road, and ran across to Helen, who had managed to stop the car just short of the ditch.

She half fell out when he opened the door.

"I'm sure I must have killed him," she wailed, and burst into tears.

"Nonsense! Listen." Two sets of moans came from the ditch, and Helen looked happier. They both noticed with relief that Tom was removing the gun from the hand of one of them.

Then they heard Tom's voice.

"Move over towards the Ford, you two. Not a movement after that. I'm in with these friendly creatures. Was in with them. They should have run to my car with the loot after the hold-up in Kingston. But they had their own car ready round a corner, and decided to cut me out. I'll ring for an ambulance to collect them. Can't have them dying on us. Why not drive to Lyme in the Ford, and report to the police there. Or, better still, leave it in a side street, and report to nobody."

Tom was now in the Rover, passing them slowly.

"Thanks for your help," he called cheerfully. "My love to Lyme," and the car sped away.

"Shall we go after him in the Ford?"

"No, Mark, no more thug-hunting just now please."

She laid her head on his shoulder, and snuggled up against his left ear.

"Let's get married instead."

Bric-à-Brac

"Second turning left, then first right, and it's a hundred yards down on your right. Can't miss it." I thanked the man and went on my way. But, as can sometimes happen, he had forgotten a mini-turning on the right before the one he wanted me to take. Eventually, finding no house with the name I was looking for, I knocked at the door of the last one on the left.

An old man, grey-haired, heavy featured and a little bent, came to the door.

"Yes," he said, upon my enquiry, "Paul Irving is an old friend, and he lives very nearby. Do you know him well?"

I shook my head. "I'm a nephew from Australia. We've never met."

"Come on in." He led me from the hall into a long ground-floor room which ran the full length of the house.

It was clearly divided into three. Study first, with desk strewn with papers and maps, walls covered with pictures of ships and yachts, and fishing tackle and waders and gloves lying around; the middle area comfortable with arm-chairs, fireplace, fine rugs and Far Eastern trifles; and further on an attractively modern dining-room with kitchen off to one side.

"Been a sailor all my life," he told me. "Like to have everything near-at-hand." He led me through sliding glass doors into the garden.

"That's where Paul lives with his daughter. There's a gate between our gardens. Let me take you across." He did so, and we approached a solid stone-built Victorian villa, with high-pitched roof and a turret at one corner. A girl came to the door, and I looked in vain at the clean-cut, friendly face for any faint resemblance to my own rough and ready features, and breathed a sigh of relief. But there was obvious pain in the frank grey eyes, and clear evidence of very recent tears.

"Oh Frank!" she said to my companion, "I'm so glad to see you. I would have come over to tell you in a few minutes. Dad had a fatal stroke a couple of hours ago. The doctor's just left, and there's nothing can be done. As you know, he had a couple of minor strokes quite recently."

She looked at me, and the smallest of smiles lightened and warmed the grey eyes as she shook my hand.

"No need to tell me who this is. Come in, both of you, please. Your room's been ready for a couple of days, David, as we weren't sure when you might arrive. But have no doubts, you are very welcome."

I helped arrange the cremation a few days later. After the service the three of us, Betty, Frank and myself, returned to her house alone, for my own family seemed to be the only relatives she had anywhere.

My uncle's will had been very simple, just a few lines leaving his house and all his possessions to his daughter.

"There's a large trunk in the attic," Betty told us. "It's always been locked. Just odds and ends, Dad told me, if I showed a touch of curiosity about it. Any idea what it could contain, Frank?"

"No," said Frank cautiously, "I've no idea really, but knowing your father for most of a lifetime, I think it might surprise us."

Up in the spacious attic, we waded through generations of bric-à-brac until we reached the window. Near it was the trunk, together with three comfortable old arm-chairs. We sat down, Betty produced a key, and after a slightly breathless hesitation, proceeded to open it.

It contained three large rectangular objects, each three or four inches thick, and carefully wrapped. There were other smaller parcels to one side.

On top lay a letter addressed in my uncle's handwriting, not simply to Betty, but to all three of us. The girl shook her head in quiet surprise, opened it slowly, and read to us.

"My dears, I hope I shall get this right. If so, I see the three of you, my dear daughter, my dear friend, and my dear brother's only son, sitting by the attic window, on dusty old chairs which I have been careful to place there just in case of such an occasion. Before you read further, Betty, would you, Frank, kindly open the package on the right in the trunk, and then a bottle of Bollinger which you will find in it. Wrapped glasses will be by the bottle. Please refresh yourselves before proceeding with this letter."

"The thoughtful old villain!" said Frank with explosive affection, as he proceeded to obey orders with practised skill.

We did not rush things, and were on our second glass before Betty turned back to the letter.

"I still very much hope to meet you, David, but it seems unlikely that such luck will come my way. This is because of an illness which only my doctor and myself know about, and which is quite separate from the strokes I've had. Increasing pain, and other things, tell me that my time is short, and that I shall soon be on my way."

Betty faltered. "Let me have it," Frank said, and took the letter.

"And now to more serious business," he read. "Your grandmother, Betty, was Josephine, second wife of Henri Rousseau, French post-impressionist, or pseudo-primitive, even surrealist as he now sometimes seems to be called. I've grown to like his vivid detail, and his unique, innocent charm. So I've been glad that three of his pictures were kept in the family, signed and unrecorded."

"Forgive my selfishness for keeping them tucked up in an attic, and never telling you of them. Trouble is, they can hardly be worth less than a million apiece. And how very tiresome to have to cope with insurance, and safeguarding the wretched things. So I gloat over and enjoy them once or twice a year, which is perhaps even better than seeing them every day."

"Your turn now," said Frank to me, "while I attend to what's left in the bottle."

There seemed little more to read, and I spoke very slowly.

"What's to do with them?" I read. "What could be simpler. I give first choice to my Betty, second to my brother's son David, and number three to my very good friend Frank. Bless you all, and there's a second bottle of bubbly below the one you must surely have finished by now."

There was a long silence when we simply sat, and thought, and felt, and said nothing. Betty was the first to break it.

"I think I'm glad that this has happened, and that Dad is finished with pain. But I'm sad that you will not meet him, David. Let's take the pictures downstairs, and look at them ourselves." She was obviously more interested in the pictures than in the Champagne, and I was more interested in her than in any of them. Frank would probably have thought well of all three.

None of us showed any wish, as yet, to consider what changes they might bring for each of us.

No unhappy ones I would think, for in a solicitor's office in Australia, there now lies the joint will of my wife Betty and myself. It states that on the death of the second of us, two pictures by Henri Rousseau shall be given to the nation by Mr. and Mrs. David Irving.

Just now, they hang in our attic, very carefully lit, and are suitably gloated over and enjoyed rather more often than once or twice a year.

What Frank has done with his picture we just don't know, and would not like to ask. Perhaps he has, rather unwillingly, found it a place among the ships and the yachts on the walls of that study of his. Almost anything could be hidden away there, quite unnoticed.